*To my beloved*
*fellow humans*

ABOUT THIS BOOK

The illustrations for this book were done in watercolor and ink on watercolor paper. This book was edited by Megan Tingley and designed by David Caplan and Kelly Brennan. The production was supervised by Ruiko Tokunaga, and the production editor was Marisa Finkelstein. The text was set in Agenda, and the display type is hand-lettered by the author.

# PING

Ani Castillo

Megan Tingley Books
LITTLE, BROWN AND COMPANY
New York   Boston

My friend,
in this life…

…we can only PING.

The PONG belongs to the other.

You Ping.

They Pong.

You Ping.

They Pong.

You might Ping a big smile.

And there are many possibilities. The Pong might be

smiling back,

getting scared,

getting angry,

or not even noticing!

Although it's good to imagine
the best
possible
Pong.

It helps to remember that
it is
not up
to you.

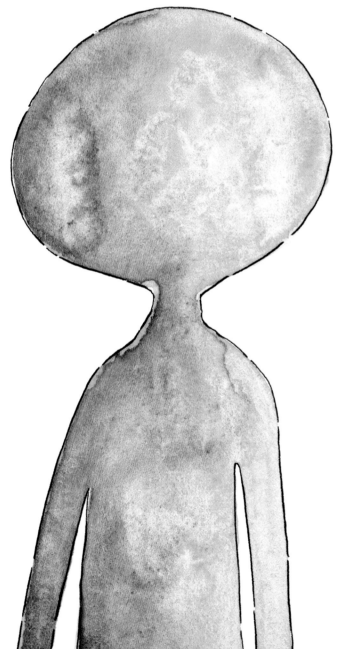

You can Ping
with your voice,

with your fingers,

with your brush.

You can Ping
through a poem,

a small gesture,

or a big one.

You can Ping by expressing feelings that just need to burst out!

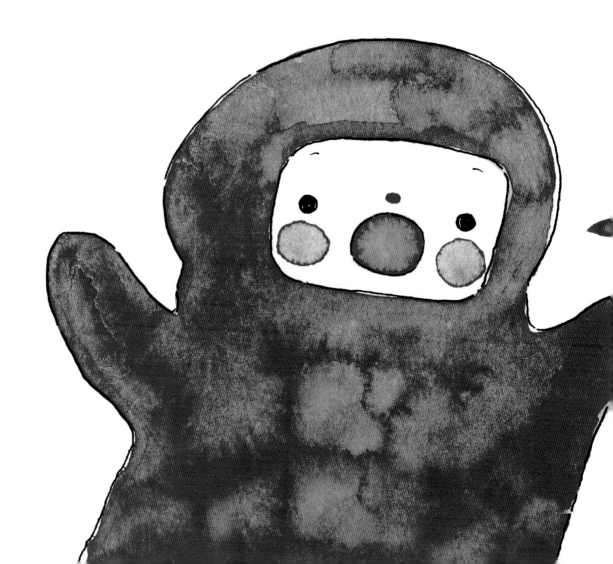

I LOVE YOU WITH A PASSION!!

You can Ping to one,

to a few,

to everyone,

to life!

You can Ping by. . .

bringing your mind,
heart, and dreams
into the real world.

To LOVE is to Ping.

To LIVE is to Ping.

# Now that you know…

curiously.

Ping freely,

generously,

Ping passionately,

bravely,

tirelessly,

and wisely.

Ping even if you're scared!

Ping adventurously,

hopefully,

joyfully.

Ping persistently,

kindly,

mindfully.

Ping far and wide.

Ping with all the love you've got!

And if you want
a lot of Pongs…

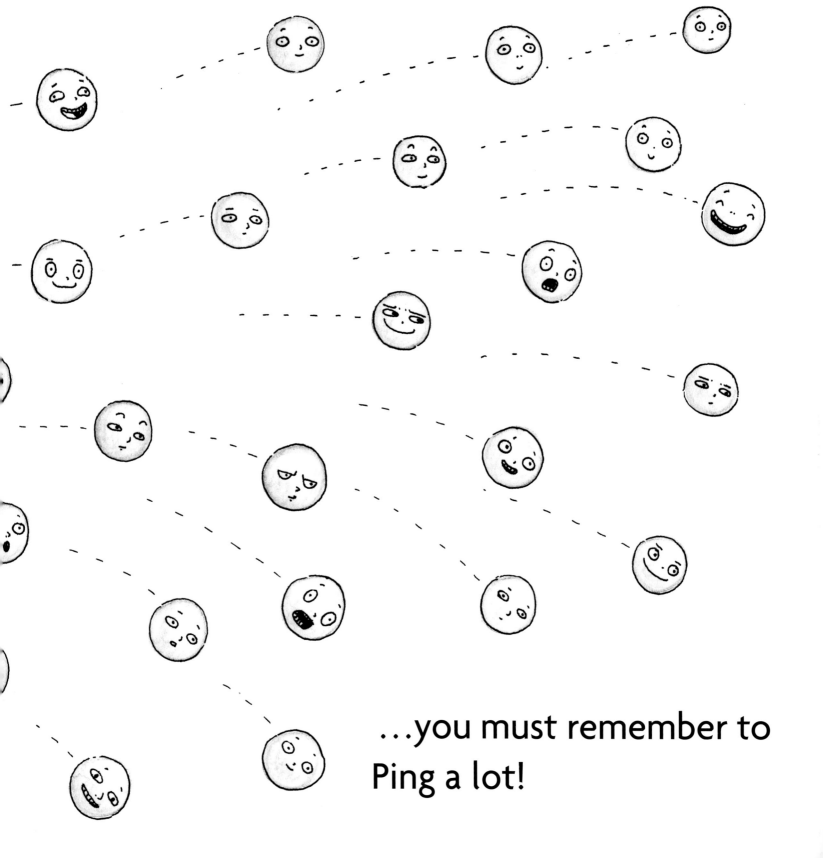

…you must remember to Ping a lot!

And then,

after you're done,

breathe deeply,
and with an open heart.

You might be ready…to receive…

# Time to listen!

The Pong is giving you something.

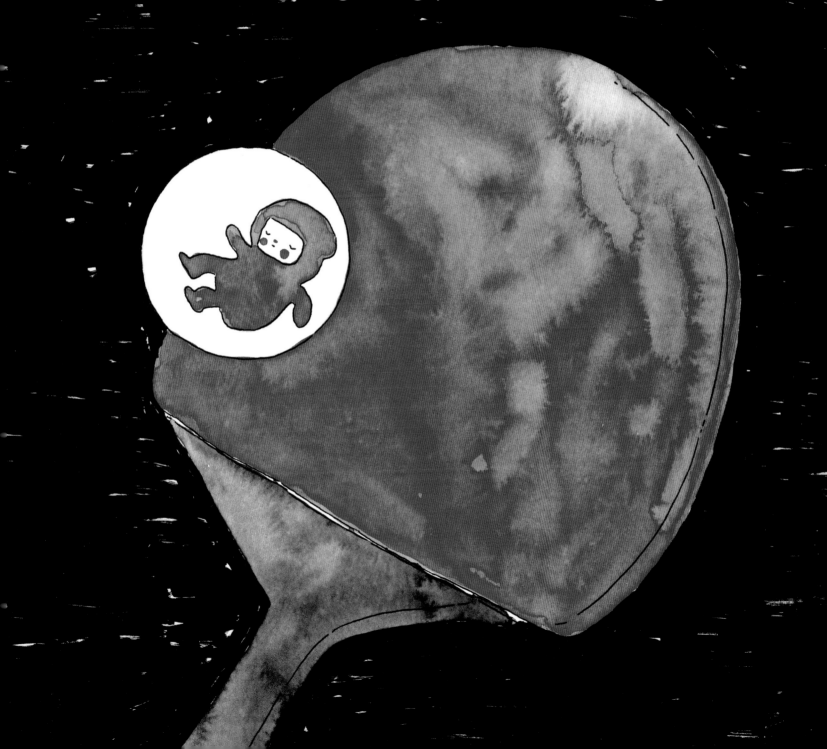

Is it something to learn?

Something to
think about?

Something to be
thankful for?

Is it something
to challenge you?

Something to keep?

Or something to let go?

You might feel like taking a pause.

It could be short…

...or as long as you need.

Now, my
dear friend,

what

will your next Ping

be?